Kim Kong

Kevin took one look at his sister, let out a wild scream, then scrambled to hide behind his dad's legs. It was Kim, sure enough, but something amazing had occurred during the night. Somehow the little girl had grown HUGE. Her head now touched the top of the doorway, and her shoulders rubbed against the side of the doorframe. She was enormous, at least seven foot tall, and due to the sudden spurt of nocturnal growth, her pyjamas had split and burst and were hanging down in tatters.

"I can't believe it!" gasped Mr Small. "My little girl!"

Also available in Young Lions

Lee Pressman

Kim Kong

Illustrated by Anni Axworthy

For Lia

First published in Great Britain in 1989 in Young Lions

Young Lions is an imprint of
the Children's Division, part of
the Collins Publishing Group,
8 Grafton Street, London W1X 3LA

Copyright © Lee Pressman 1989
© Illustrations Anni Axworthy 1989

Printed and bound in Great Britain by
William Collins Sons & Co. Ltd, Glasgow

1
Gro-Kwik

Kim Small had a big problem and his name was Kevin. Kim was seven years old. She had curly hair (she wished it was straight), a wobbly front tooth (she wished *that* would drop out) and she was extremely kind to animals.

Kevin Small (her big brother) was twelve. He was tall and skinny with spiky black hair and a fierce temper. He was always angry about something and the thing that made him most angry was having a kid sister.

Kevin hated the way his dad and his uncles and aunts all fussed over Kim. He hated it when his friends came round and said how cute Kim was. He hated all her silly toys. He hated it when she sang in the bath. He even hated her wobbly tooth. But the thing he hated most of all was having to collect Kim from school every day. When they walked back along the street, he always made her walk a few paces behind so that nobody would

know they were together and he'd give her a hard pinch if she wandered too close.

Having a big bully for a brother was an awful problem for Kim. She didn't know what to do about it.

One Thursday afternoon Kevin arrived home from school. He threw his reading book on the floor and, still wearing his coat, collapsed on the sofa and flicked on the television. Three cheesey grins appeared on the screen. They belonged to Ziggy, Wiggy and Arthur, the presenters of the extremely popular kids' TV show, *Splodge*.

"Hi there!" giggled Wiggy breathlessly, "and welcome to another action packed prog. Later on, Arthur will be showing you how to make your very own personal computer out of three empty Crunchybix packets, a cardboard tube, two yoghurt cartons and a length of strong elastic. But first, over to Ziggy who this week's been discovering the joys of underwater nose wrestling..."

At that moment Kim arrived home. She shut the front door, took off her coat and hung it neatly in the cupboard under the stairs.

"I'm thirsty," she said, entering the sitting room. "I need a drink."

"Well, go and get one then!" said Kevin unpleasantly, not taking his eyes from the screen.

Kim wandered across the room and sat down at the table. She peered over at the television.

"Can't we watch the other side?" she asked. "You always watch *Splodge*. There's a cartoon on the other side I'd like to see."

"No!" snapped Kevin. "I'm watching this. It's my favourite programme."

Kim sighed. At that moment she looked down

at the table and noticed a cup. She peered into it and saw it contained a sparkling green liquid.

"Look, Kevin," she said, "Dad's left a drink out."

It was not unusual for Kim and Kevin's dad to leave a drink or a snack out for the children when they returned home from school. Kim picked up the cup and put it to her lips. She took a long deep gulp.

"Give me some," ordered Kevin from the sofa, but Kim had had enough of his bossiness.

"No!" she said indignantly. "Why should I? You wouldn't even share your crisps on the way home." Defiantly she swallowed the last drops and wiped her mouth on the back of her hand. Kevin (who hadn't really wanted a drink at all) turned his attention back to the television.

Kim put down the cup. She licked her lips. She'd never had anything quite like that before. It didn't taste bad, it had a fizzy fruity flavour, but now she'd finished it she began to feel a bit odd. She didn't feel ill or sick but she definitely knew that something strange was starting to happen inside her. It began with a feeling like pins and needles which started at the top of her head then went tingling right down her spine to the tips of her toes. Then the tickly prickly feeling was replaced by an itching and a scratching all over her body but on the inside not on the outside of her skin. When that stopped she felt a burpy, slurpy, squelchy, belchy, muzzy, fuzzy, rushing and gushing sensation that made her feel burning hot then freezing cold then hot then cold then hot again, but all in the space of a second.

While all this extraordinary activity was going on inside Kim, Kevin sat glued to the box, quite unaware of what was happening.

The door opened. Kim and Kevin's dad came in from the kitchen, struggling with a watering can, full to the brim, which he slopped across the carpet and thumped down hard on the table.

"Hi there, you two," he smiled. "Good day at school?"

Kevin went on watching the TV and said nothing.

Kim tried to reply but instead only a loud "HIC!" emerged from her lips.

"Well, don't all talk at once," said Mr Small.

Kim stood up. Her legs felt rather wobbly, but apart from that the effects of the drink seemed to have passed. It was at this point that Mr Small noticed the empty cup. He picked it up and looked at it bewildered. The smile fell from his face.

"Where's all this gone then?" he barked, turning to Kevin for an explanation.

"Don't look at me!" said Kevin. "Ask greedy guts over there. She drank it."

Mr Small's face turned a ghostly grey.

"She did what?" he gasped.

"Is there any more in the fridge, Dad?" asked Kevin. "I didn't get any. I'm gasping."

"She *drank* it!" cried Mr Small with such a horrified shriek that both Kim and Keven knew for sure that something serious had happened.

"I'm sorry, Dad," whispered Kim. "Was it yours? I didn't mean to drink *your* drink."

"It wasn't *my* drink!" shouted Mr Small. "It wasn't anybody's drink! It wasn't a drink at all!"

"W...w...well, what was it then if it wasn't a drink?" stuttered Kim, beginning to feel a bit worried by the way her dad was carrying on.

Mr Small took a large green bottle down from the shelf and held it up. He read out what was written on the label:

**Gro-Kwik the wonder plant tonic. You too
can have peas the size of pumpkins.**

"It's a plantfood," he said, "very powerful plantfood. I bought it to try and make my tomatoes
grow bigger."

A snigger followed by a burst of laughter came
from the direction of the sofa. Kevin was enjoying the situation, especially the look of discomfort
on his little sister's face.

Mr Small continued, "The instructions said
mix one cup of concentrated *Gro-Kwik* with a
gallon of water. I measured out one cupful of the
liquid. I went into the kitchen for the water and...
and..."

"And *she* guzzled it all!" laughed Kevin spite-
fully. "What a joke! Ha ha ha ha ha."

He laughed so much that he rolled off the sofa
on to the carpet.

"It's not funny!" shouted Mr Small. "This is
serious."

Kevin had to stuff a cushion over his mouth to
stop himself howling. Tears of laughter ran down
his face.

Mr Small looked closely at Kim and put his

hand on her forehead. Then he touched her wrist and attempted to locate her pulse. He wasn't a medical man but he'd seen doctors do this sort of thing on the television.

"You just sit down, girl," he said. "Now, how do you feel? Any pains? Stomach ache? Feel sick?"

"I'm OK," smiled Kim taking her dad's hand. "Honestly. I did feel a bit strange at first but I'm fine now. You can stop worrying."

"I'm not taking any chances," said Mr Small gravely. "We're going along to the hospital to have you checked out thoroughly. Kevin... Kim... Coats."

"But Dad," groaned Kevin. "I'm watching telly. Why do *I* have to come? Just because that stupid twit's gone and guzzled some grotty green gunge, I've got to miss my favourite programme. It's not fair!"

"KEVIN!!! For once just do as you're told!" bellowed Mr Small. "Your sister might have poisoned herself. She's just drunk a cup of concentrated *Gro-Kwik*! We've got to get her to the hospital immediately. Who knows what might happen to her?"

2

The Big Foot

Dr Patel pulled back the curtains and smiled.

"Well, Mr Small," she began, "good news. I've examined your daughter from top to toe, and I can't find anything wrong with her."

"Phew! What a relief!" said Mr Small. "I was beginning to get a bit worried."

The Smalls had been at the hospital for two and a half hours. Kevin had stayed in the waiting room reading a comic while behind the curtain in the small cubicle Dr Patel had been making a most thorough examination of Kim.

"You're a very lucky little girl," said the doctor, patting her on the head. "In future you must never never never drink anything when you don't know what it is."

"I won't," said Kim. "I promise."

"My fault really," said Mr Small guiltily. "I should never have left that wretched stuff there in the first place."

"Indeed," said the doctor sternly. "By the way, Mr Small, you don't happen to have the plant food with you by any chance do you?"

Mr Small dug his hand deep into his jacket pocket and pulled out the half-filled bottle of *Gro-Kwik* which he handed to the doctor.

"I'd like to examine this in the lab," she explained, "just to make absolutely sure that it's not harmful."

Mr Small and Kim thanked Dr Patel for her help and then walked out into the waiting room.

"You've been a long time," said Kevin. "I've read this flippin' comic six times."

"Your sister had to have lots of tests done," explained Mr Small, "x-rays, blood samples, all that stuff."

"Hmpf!" snorted Kevin, obviously not impressed.

The Smalls walked out of the warm hospital into the cool night air. Mr Small held Kim's hand as they crossed the forecourt while Kevin slouched along a few paces behind. Mr Small passed by the long line of cars and stopped by a large red lorry that was taking up six spaces in the hospital car park. He took a heavy bunch of keys from his pocket and unlocked the door of the cab. He lifted Kim up the steep step then went to give Kevin a hand.

"I can manage!" snapped Kevin, "why can't we have a car like other people?"

It was true that Mr Small didn't have a car, but his job as a lorry driver meant he could often bring home his lorry and use it whenever he wanted.

The big red truck chugged along the busy city streets and soon they were crossing the River Thames and passing Big Ben. Kim looked up at the vast illuminated clock face.

"Eight o'clock." she said.

"Time you two had something to eat," said Mr Small, clunking the heavy gearstick into third. "Tell you what, we'll grab some chips on the way home, then as soon as we get back it'll be bath and bed."

Everyone felt better after they'd eaten; by nine o'clock Kim and Kevin were in their pyjamas and climbing into their beds. Kevin moaned and groaned about not being allowed to watch the television but Mr Small insisted that it was far too late for all that. By half past nine the children were asleep. Downstairs, Mr Small sank grate-fully into an armchair to read his newspaper.

*

Kevin woke up on Friday morning to hear his dad calling him from the bathroom. "Time to get up, Kevin! Come on, it's getting late. Go and wake your sister, please. I'm in the middle of shaving."

This was another job that Kevin resented. Kim was a particularly heavy sleeper and he'd often have to spend five minutes trying to rouse her in the morning. She'd be lying there all tucked up and cosy, buried under a sea of furry teddies and cuddly rabbits. Sometimes he felt an urge to throw a bucket of cold water over her. That would certainly have got her moving, but he knew his dad wouldn't appreciate the joke.

Kevin stood outside Kim's door and tried banging with his fist.

"Wake up in there! Time for school!" he shouted.

There was no reply nor sound of movement from inside the room. Kevin tutted to himself and pushed the door open.

The curtains were still drawn, the room was in darkness and at first everything appeared the same as it always was. But just as he was about to approach the bed and shout in Kim's ear, Kevin stopped and listened. From under the duvet came a loud rasping snore. It was a snore so loud and so deep that he found it difficult to believe that his little sister could be making it. Kevin shrugged his shoulders and walked towards the end of the bed. It was then that he saw something that made his blood run cold. Sticking out from beneath the duvet was a foot. Nothing strange in that you may

say but this was a big foot, a very big foot, bigger than Kevin's foot and it certainly did not belong to Kim.

Kevin's mouth suddenly felt like the bottom of a bird cage. His knees had turned to rubber. He tried to call out for his dad but no sound came from his lips.

The giant foot gave a twitch and disappeared under the covers. Kevin felt sick with fright. His guts were churning. He slowly began to back away, step by step towards the open bedroom door. He'd almost made it when...

"SQUARK!!!"

Kevin screamed.

He'd stepped on Kim's squeaky toy duck that was lying on the carpet. There was a rustling from the bed and a large figure began to toss and turn.

This was all too much for Kevin. He stumbled out of the bedroom, dashed wildly along the landing and fell into the bathroom.

Mr Small stood in front of the mirror, his face covered in shaving cream. He gave Kevin a puzzled look and went on delicately scraping his whiskers.

"Have you woken Kim up yet?" he asked between scrapes.

"DAD!!!" shrieked Kevin. "You've got to come quick! There's someone in Kim's bed. I dunno who or what it is, a burglar or a monster or something but whatever it is... it's BIG!!!"

Mr Small was not amused.

"Burglar? Monster? Ha! I've told you, Kevin, you watch too much telly. You fill yourself up with all that rubbish, then you start imagining things."

"I didn't imagine anything!" cried Kevin. "I heard it, horrible snoring and roaring. I saw it as well!"

"Well, what did you see exactly?" asked Mr Small with a disbelieving chuckle.

"I saw a big foot sticking out of the bed," gasped Kevin. Mr Small laughed.

"Is this one of your silly jokes, Kevin?" he said. "I've heard of Bigfoot. Or perhaps it's the yeti or maybe even the Loch Ness Monster."

"Oh Dad!" cried Kevin. "Why won't you believe me?"

At that moment they both heard footsteps outside on the landing.

"There's your sister now," said Mr Small.

"Kim!" he called out to his daughter. "What have you been doing to frighten your brother? He's scared out of his wits. Come into the bathroom a moment, will you?"

The footsteps approached and the bathroom door was flung wide open. Mr Small turned. Suddenly his eyes popped and his heart nearly stopped when he gazed at the incredible figure that stood there before him.

3
Kim Kong

"Morning, Dad," said Kim smiling sweetly.

Kevin took one look at his sister, let out a wild scream, then scrambled to hide behind his dad's legs. Mr Small dropped his razor and goggled with disbelief at his daughter. It was Kim, sure enough, there was no doubt of that, but something amazing had occurred during the night. Somehow the little girl had grown HUGE. Her head now touched the top of the doorway, and her shoulders rubbed against the side of the doorframe. She was enormous, at least seven foot tall, and due to the sudden spurt of nocturnal growth, her pyjamas had split and burst and were hanging down in tatters.

"I can't believe it!" gasped Mr Small. "My little girl!"

Kevin was on the floor sobbing and whimpering.

"Tell her to go away," he begged. "I don't like it."

"Pull yourself together, boy," snapped Mr Small. "It's only your sister."

"What's happened to me, Dad?" asked Kim, trying to look at herself in the bathroom mirror. "I'm so big."

"It must be that *Gro-Kwik* mixture," exclaimed Mr Small. "Now don't panic. Don't panic! I'd better call Dr Patel and let her know what's happened."

Mr Small tried to leave the bathroom but Kevin clung terrified to his leg and was dragged crying and screaming across the floor.

"Let go!" shouted Mr Small. "I've got to phone the hospital. Why don't you both get ready for school?"

"But what am I going to wear, Dad?" asked Kim. "None of my clothes will fit me any more."

Mr Small thought for a moment. "Er... um?... Go and get something from my wardrobe. I might have something big enough."

So while Mr Small phoned Dr Patel and Kevin scuttled off to hide in his room, Kim went into her dad's bedroom and looked through his clothes. She eventually found some pants, socks, a T-shirt, an old pair of jeans and some trainers. Even these weren't really big enough for her but she managed to squeeze into them somehow.

Meanwhile Mr Small had got through to Dr Patel at the hospital and was excitedly explaining what had happened to Kim during the night. The doctor listened with great interest then said:

"Well, Mr Small, there's really nothing I can do for your daughter at this moment. I'll get cracking in the lab analysing the *Gro-Kwik* and hopefully I'll be able to come up with another mixture, an antidote, to bring her back to her normal size."

"But what about Kim in the meantime?" asked Mr Small fearfully.

"Well," explained the doctor, "all this is going to take some time. We can't rush these things. I suggest you and your family just try and make the best of it and carry on as usual."

Mr Small looked thoughtful as he put down the phone. Surely in these modern times of computers, and microchips with everything, it shouldn't take long to come up with a shrinking solution. Still in a daze, he wandered into the kitchen to prepare the children's breakfast. Kim was the first one ready. Dressed in her dad's clothes she shuffled in and sat at the table. All that growing in the night had made her ravenous.

Upstairs, Kevin too was feeling peckish. As he looked round his room at his colourful posters of superheroes doing battle with fiendish seven-headed intergalactic space dragons he felt ashamed that he'd been so scared of his own kid sister. Summoning up what courage he had left, he dressed and came down for breakfast. By the time he reached the kitchen, Kim had already devoured three bowls of Crunchybix Cereal, two plates of egg and bacon, five slices of toast and marmalade, four cups of tea, and a bowl of steaming hot porridge.

"What an appetite!" beamed Mr Small, dishing up a huge platter of fried bread and baked beans. Kevin held up the empty Crunchybix packet in disgust.

"Cor! She's scoffed the lot!" he moaned. "Flippin' cheek."

Now he'd got over his initial shock at seeing his sister so huge, Kevin was starting to find the new enlarged Kim even more annoying than the old little one.

After breakfast Mr Small explained that although the situation was rather strange, they must try to continue as normal.

"That means I'm going to go off to work in my lorry as usual, and you two are going to go to school," he said.

"But what's everyone going to say when they see that hulking great monster?" asked Kevin unkindly.

Mr Small gave his son a hard frown. "Look, Kevin, she's your little sister no matter what's happened to her and it's your responsibility to look after her. Now collect your books and get off to school."

Kevin put on his coat, Kim borrowed one of her dad's jackets, and the children left the house. For the first time ever Kevin found it impossible to make Kim walk behind him. She had such long legs that she kept catching him up all the time.

All their schoolfriends were astounded by Kim's transformation. One by one they ran up and gasped with astonishment when they clapped eyes on Kevin's seven-foot sister. Before long a whole crowd of kids had attached itself to Kim and Kevin, all firing questions and some even pinching Kim to make sure she was real.

"Wow! What've you been feeding her on then, Kev?"

"What did you do, Kev? Blow her up with a bicycle pump?"

"Think your sister needs to go on a drastic diet, Kev."

Kim smiled and took it all very well. Kevin hated all the fuss and attention. He felt deeply embarrassed and humiliated by his dopey giant of a sister.

As they all arrived at the gates of the school, some of the followers-on began shouting and teasing Kim and hurling nasty insults at her. Now, some brothers, hearing their only sister being taunted like this, would have rushed to their defence. Not Kevin. He'd already decided to join in with his pals so he began to jeer along with everyone else. In fact he caused the biggest laugh of all when he shouted out:

"Well, you lot, what do you think of my new sister then? Say goodbye to Kim Small, say hello to KIM KONG!"

All Kevin's friends fell about laughing.

"Kim Kong!" they shrieked. "Kim Kong!"

The school bell interrupted their merriment. There was a general scattering in all directions as everyone raced for their classrooms.

Kim stood alone in the playground. She was feeling very mixed up and confused. Yesterday she'd been an ordinary little girl. Yesterday her main concern had been her loose tooth. But today was different. Today she was enormous and strong. Today she was Kim Kong.

4

Billy the Bully

As the sound of the school bell died away, Kim set off for her classroom. She reached the door and ducked down to enter the room. All the children giggled and pointed as the giant girl hung up her dad's jacket then came over to sit on the mat in the reading corner. It was difficult to bend and cross her long legs without nudging and kneeing her classmates in the back. When she was finally sitting comfortably, she towered head and shoulders above everyone else.

Ms Keady, the teacher, sat on her chair with the register on her lap. She at least was not surprised to see the enormous girl as Mr Small had already phoned the school and told her all about Kim's unusual predicament.

"Good morning, everybody," smiled Ms Keady. "Now I'm just going to call the register."

She opened the book, and took out her red and black pens, and began to shout out the names:

"Sandy."

"Here, Miss."

"Tracey."

"Here, Miss."

"Nirad."

"Here, Miss Keady."

"Errol."

"Yes, Miss."

Ms Keady continued down the list in alphabetical order. Eventually she called,

"Kim."

But before Kim had a chance to answer, somebody else shouted out: "Kong!"

All the children thought this was wildly funny and began to shriek with laughter. Ms Keady did not laugh. She slammed the register shut and glared at the class. One of Ms Keady's scorching glares was enough to stun an ox. All the children fell suddenly silent.

"Listen to me, everybody," began the teacher, "and listen carefully. What's happened to Kim is very unfortunate but it could just as easily have happened to anyone. Some people are tall. Others are small. Some people are fat. Others are thin. Everybody's different in their own way and in my class we do not make fun of people who are 'different'. Understood? I don't want to hear any more of this nonsense. Do I make myself clear?"

"Yes, Miss," mumbled the class.

"Good," said Ms Keady. "Let's get back to the register and then we'll get down to some work."

The morning proceeded peacefully. The children continued with their dinosaur project, writing in their folders and doing paintings and drawings of those giant monsters of long ago.

Kim was now too large to sit at one of the small tables and the class were madly jealous when Ms Keady allowed her to work at the teacher's desk.

It was playtime when the real trouble began. At the sound of the mid-morning bell, the children put on their coats and filed out into the play-ground for a fifteen minute break. Two of Kim's best friends, Tracey and Stacey, asked her if she'd like to play skipping with them. Kim said she'd love to and the three girls went off to play quietly in the corner of the playground. They had a lovely game although when it was Kim's turn to skip, the two little girls found it a bit difficult to spin the rope high enough for her. But they still

managed to have fun, and were bothering no one, when suddenly, for no reason at all, one of the big boys, Billy Wilkinson, ambled over and propped himself up against the wall to watch them.

Billy was a tough character – or at least he liked to think he was. He had a porky little face, beady little eyes and cropped hair like a lavatory brush. To keep up his tough image, he had tattoos of skulls, crudely drawn in felt-tipped pen, on the back of each hand.

Billy chewed his gum and scowled. A crowd of

his cronies followed him over and stood loyally round their hero. They didn't particularly like Billy but they were too terrified of him not to be in his gang.

After a moment, Billy opened his mouth, which resembled a slot in a letter box, and began to chant sneeringly:

> "Kim Kong, Kim Kong,
> Your knickers are too long.
> Bet your smelly socks pong.
> Kim Kong, Kim Kong."

All Billy's mates hooted with laughter and patted Billy on the back.

"Don't take any notice of him," said Tracey.

"He's just a big bully," said Stacey.

"Let's just ignore him and get on with our game," said Kim. And they did.

Now if there was one thing that Billy couldn't stand it was being ignored. When he started something he only wanted it to end in trouble. So he began singing again but this time louder:

> "Kim Kong, Kim Kong,
> Your knickers are too long.

Bet your smelly socks pong,
Kim Kong, Kim Kong."

At the end of the verse Kim stopped skipping and walked over to Billy. Billy hadn't realised quite how big Kim really was until she was towering over him. He would have backed away and made a run for it if he hadn't been standing against the wall and unable to move. Sweating madly and desperately flattening himself against the bricks, Billy looked up at the enormous girl.

"You d..d...don't scare me, you monster!" he stuttered.

"And you don't scare me either," smiled Kim. "Sticks and stones may break my bones but names can never hurt me."

Tracey and Stacey clapped with delight. Kim turned and walked back to her friends. As they began skipping again, Billy plucked up enough courage for one final retort:

"Monster!" he shouted before he beetled away to hide behind the sheds to plan his next move.

Billy was shaking with rage. He felt desperate. He had to do something to show his gang that he was still tops. He had to show off his strength and courage. An evil smile came to his lips. Across the playground getting a drink at the water fountain was Kevin Small. Well, if Billy couldn't put the frighteners on Kim then he would certainly scare the living daylights out of her weedy jelly of a brother, Kevin.

Adopting the same approach that had got him nowhere with Kim, Billy walked over to the drinking fountain and began to chant behind Kevin's back:

"Kev the shrimp, Kev the shrimp,
Your sister's blown up like a blimp.
But you're a weedy little wimp.
Kev the shrimp, Kev the shrimp."

"Oh, shut up, Wilkinson!" snapped Kevin. "Leave me alone."

"Ooooh! Did you hear that, lads?" called out Billy. "Didn't you like my little song then, Smallfry? Tell you what, I'll sing it again."

And he did:

"Kev the shrimp, Kev the shrimp,
Your sister's blown up like a blimp.
But you're a weedy little wimp.
Kev the shrimp, Kev the shrimp."

This was all too much for Kevin. He was feeling wretched enough as it was. He'd had about all the teasing he could take. Hardly knowing what he was doing he threw himself at Billy. This was just what Billy wanted – a punch up! He grabbed Kevin by the hair and swung him over to one side. Kevin fell to the ground but bobbed up like a cork in a bottle to land a quick punch on Billy's chin.

By now a crowd was forming in a big circle round the two boys. Shouts of encouragement came from the sea of excited faces.

"Fight! Fight!"

"Let him have it, Kev!"

"Smash him, Billy!"

"Do him over!"

Tracey, Stacey and Kim stopped their game when they saw all the activity at the far end of the playground.

"What's happening?" asked Tracey.

"Let's go and see," said Stacey.

The two small girls and their tall friend rushed across to find out what was going on.

"I can't see a thing," shouted Tracey trying to wriggle her way through the crowd.

Kim, of course, being so tall, had a perfect view over the heads of the other children. As soon as she saw what was happening, a great anger rose up inside her.

Billy now had Kevin on the ground and was sitting on top of him, twisting his ears and laughing every time Kevin screamed. Billy was enjoying himself so much that he didn't notice what was going on just behind him. The crowd suddenly parted as Kim launched herself forwards. With a hand the size of a bunch of bananas, she picked up Billy the bully by the scruff of the neck and lifted him four feet off the ground. The bewildered boy screamed in terror. His legs thrashed about wildly, trying in vain to give Kim a kick. As she was holding him at arm's length, there was no way that he could reach her.

"Let me down!" blubbed Billy. "I'm telling on you! I'll get my dad up here! He'll make mincemeat of you! He does karate, you know! He's got a black belt!"

"Well..." retorted Kim, "my dad's got red braces."

The crowd screamed with laughter. It was a real treat seeing Billy getting a taste of his own

medicine. On the wall just above Kim's head was a sturdy hook where a lamp had once been fixed. Kim raised her arm and lifted Billy up a bit higher. With a flourish she looped the hood of his anorak over the hook and left the boy dangling there. Billy was completely stuck halfway up the wall. He wriggled and jiggled and sobbed and howled but there was no way he could get down.

Just then Mr Crump, the headteacher, managed to push his way through the cheering crowd. Even he had to stifle a grin when he saw Billy hanging there like a limp string puppet.

"I suppose you did this," he said turning to Kim.

"Sorry, Mr Crump," apologised Kim. "He was beating up my brother."

"Yes, well, that wouldn't surprise me a bit," sighed Mr Crump. "But you'd better get him down now, Kim. I think he's had enough."

Kim reached up, unhooked Billy and lowered him to the ground. He looked quite a sight. He was sobbing and crying and rubbing his eyes. His tears had made the felt-tipped skulls on the back of his hands go all splodgy and in his attempt to dry his face he'd smudged black ink all over his cheeks.

"I'll get my dad on to you!" he bellowed. "And my mum and my big brother and his dog..."

"Don't forget your grannie's budgie," called a voice from the crowd and everyone hooted with laughter. Billy's threats died away as Mr Crump led him off to the medical room for a quiet sit down and a nice drink of milk. The circle of children broke up and Kim went across to her brother.

"You all right, Kevin?" she asked with concern.

"'Course I'm all right, Dopey!" he said ungratefully. "I dunno why you had to come over and stick your big nose in. I almost had him beaten."

"Well, I thought..." began Kim, but she got no further.

"Oh, leave me alone," snapped Kevin. "Just go away and leave me alone!" And with his hands in his pockets, Kevin turned away and walked grumpily off to join in the football game.

5

A Home for Kim

After the Billy Wilkinson incident, Kim's day at school passed without further trouble. Lunch was a problem, as Mrs Sugg, the school cook, wasn't quite sure what to give a seven-foot girl with the appetite of an elephant, but eventually she scraped together enough food and Kim didn't go hungry.

At home time Kim waited by the gate for her brother. As Kevin approached he looked up at his sister suspiciously.

"You've grown," he said suddenly. "You've definitely got bigger."

"Do you think so?" asked Kim.

"I know so," said Kevin. "This morning I came up to your waist. Now I only come up to your knee."

"Oh no!" sighed Kim. "I hoped I wasn't going to get any bigger. But I thought my clothes were beginning to feel a bit tight."

When the children turned into their street they saw their dad's lorry parked in front of the house. Mr Small was standing by the gate and he came up to meet them.

"You've got bigger," he gasped.

"That's what I said," said Kevin.

"What are we going to do, Dad?" asked Kim fearfully. "I don't think I'll be able to get in the house."

Kim was right. She was now twelve feet tall and still growing. Manoeuvring through normal doorways had become impossible. Mr Small scratched his head.

"We're going to have to find you somewhere else to live, temporarily, of course, until you're back to your proper size. Now let's think... Any ideas, Kevin?"

"The elephant house at London Zoo?" suggested Kevin maliciously.

"No. That's no good," replied Mr Small seriously. "What about the smell?"

"The elephants would get used to her," said Kevin.

"How about an aircraft hangar?" said Mr Small. "They're huge."

"Wouldn't it be a bit noisy, Dad?" asked Kim. "I'd never be able to get to sleep."

Kevin began to get fed up with the conversation.

"This is ridiculous!" he snorted. "We can't do anything with her. She should be in the circus."

Mr Small rubbed his chin thoughtfully. "The circus..." he muttered. "The circus... THE CIRCUS!"

Suddenly his face lit up.

"Brilliant idea, Kevin. Well done."

"I was only joking," said Kevin.

"No, no. It's a real brainwave," exclaimed his dad. "You remember, years ago when you were a little kid, I used to drive a lorry for Perry Pottle?"

"Perry Pottle the circus owner?" gasped Kim.

"That's the man," beamed Mr Small. "Perry and me used to get on famously. I bet if I phoned him up and told him what's happened, he'd lend me one of his Big Top tents. He's got several of them, you know. We could pitch it in the park over the road so you wouldn't be far away."

"Well, I'm not sure," began Kim nervously.

"It's worth a try," cried Mr Small. "I'll get on the phone right away." With that he rushed into

the house and began flicking through the phone book for Perry Pottle's number. Kevin followed his dad inside and threw himself on to the sofa to watch the telly. Kim, who was too big to fit through the front door, waited in the garden, watching the TV through the sitting-room window.

After ten minutes Mr Small reappeared with a huge smile on his face.

"I've spoken to Perry Pottle and he said he'd be delighted to bring over a spare Big Top for you to sleep in tonight, Kim. That's great, isn't it?"

Kim nodded and grinned.

"Now I've just got to phone the council and get permission to put the tent up in the park."

Mr Small went back into the hall and picked up the telephone again.

6

Perry Pottle Lends a Hand

Now, as you can imagine, trying to keep a twelve-foot girl a secret is impossible. Everyone at school had seen Kim, they'd all told their mums and dads and grannies and grandads and aunties and uncles and they'd all told their friends and neighbours and they'd all told *their* friends and their friend's friends and their friend's friend's friends and before very long, half the people in town had heard about the incredible growing girl from 37 Park Road.

Lots of people who heard about it didn't believe it and wanted to see for themselves if it could really be true. So, before very long, Kim noticed various faces bobbing up over the hedge trying to get a good look at her. Being a friendly sort of girl she waved back at the people who at first were too startled to respond. A baby took one look at Kim and burst out crying. Two dogs began to howl.

More people arrived. They came in cars, on

bikes, and in taxis, and the road began to get quite congested outside the Smalls' house. Crowds started to gather on the pavement and everyone agreed they'd never seen anything quite like it before.

Kevin was still sprawled out on the sofa but soon even he began to notice the cheers and the chatter, the commotion and the buzz of excitement outside.

"What's all the racket?" he bellowed, sticking his head out of the window. "I can hardly hear the telly."

"Just some people come to see me," smiled Kim. "Some of them asked for my autograph, you know."

"Tell them to shut up! It's getting on my nerves," complained Kevin. But Kim did no such thing. She was much too polite. She waved to the people and posed for their photographs and explained to the reporter from the newspaper just how it felt to be LONDON'S LARGEST LASS. It wasn't long before the television cameras arrived and camera crews started busily erecting scaffolding in the front garden so they could get really good shots of Kim for the six o'clock news.

Children climbed lamp-posts to get a better view. Hotdog stands appeared. The police arrived and tried in vain to unblock the street which was now jam-packed with tourists and sightseers arriving by the coachload.

Mr Small finally finished making his phone call. It had taken a long time and much hard persuasion to get the council to agree to having the Big Top in the park but since no performing animals or dangerous stunts were involved they eventually said yes. As Mr Small opened his front door to step outside and tell Kim the good news, twenty flashguns went off in his face.

"Cor! What's going on?" he gasped.

"You must be Kim's dad," said a lady with a microphone. "What does it feel like to be the father of a giant?"

But Mr Small didn't have a chance to answer. Just at that moment a great cheer went up from the crowd. An enormous, gaily painted lorry was trying to wend its way through the people and parked cars. A large speaker on top of the lorry was blasting out loud brass-band music. Sitting at the driving wheel of the cab was a ruddy-faced man with a curly moustache and a top hat.

"It's Perry Pottle!" shouted Mr Small. "He's arrived with the tent. Hooray!"

Kim's dad ran down the garden path and forced his way past the balloon sellers and hot-chestnut stands into the middle of the road. Perry Pottle leapt down from his lorry and the two men hugged each other warmly.

"Great to see you, Mr Pottle."

"Great to see you too, Ken," laughed the circus man, slapping his old friend heartily on the back. "Now you must introduce me to this marvellous daughter of yours."

Mr Small led Perry Pottle through the crowds and into the front garden.

"Perry Pottle at your service," said the circus man, taking off his top hat and bowing.

"Hello," said Kim. "Thank you for letting me use your Big Top."

"My pleasure, young lady," replied Perry Pottle. "And if you ever want a job in my circus just let me know right away. You'd be a sensation!"

"It's getting dark," said Mr Small. "Shouldn't we start getting the tent up now?"

"Indeedy, indeedy," chuckled Perry Pottle. "Now, come on everyone. Let's get this show on the road."

Perry Pottle had brought along a dozen of his circus workers and by the spotlights of the camera crews they started to put up the Big Top in the park opposite Kim's house.

It was exciting to watch the enormous blue-and-white striped tent rise up into the night sky and even Kevin broke off from watching the TV to creep upstairs to have a peep from the top bedroom window.

While all this busy bustle of activity was going

on, Kim was beginning to feel hungry. Perry Pottle generously went over to one of the vans and bought fifty hamburgers. One for Mr Small, one for Kevin, and forty-eight for Kim.

As evening fell, what with the lights and the music and the smell of toffee apples and candy floss, there was quite a carnival atmosphere outside 37 Park Road. The tent was now up and Perry Pottle showed Kim her new home.

"What do you think then, young lady?" he smiled.

"It's great, Mr Pottle. Thank you very much," said Kim.

"One thing before I go," said the circus man. "You're all invited to my grand funfair tomorrow morning. Ten o'clock, Clapham Common. See you there." And with a cheery wave, Perry Pottle climbed back in his truck and was off.

Most of the neighbours lent Kim their spare blankets, sheets, cushions and duvets and a large comfortable bed was arranged in the middle of the tent. Kim crawled under the snug covers feeling extremely tired. Her head was spinning as she thought over all the strange events of the day. When Mr Small came to kiss her goodnight he noticed that she was looking unhappy.

"Stop worrying, love," he smiled. "You've had something to eat, you've got somewhere to sleep and Dr Patel's working on an antidote to the *Gro-Kwik*."

"I know all that, Dad," said Kim, "but that's not what I'm worrying about. What frightens me is if I grow any more during the night, I'll have nothing big enough to wear for school tomorrow."

7

ACE!

The problem of what Kim was to wear was solved the next morning in a most unexpected way. At 7 a.m. Mr Small crossed the road to wake his daughter up with a nice hot bucket of tea. All the crowds had long since gone, leaving behind them a sea of litter scattered across the street.

As Mr Small picked his way through the crisp packets and cola cans, he noticed an enormous limousine parked in front of the Big Top. It was so long it looked as if three ordinary cars had been welded together to make one huge one. The windows of the car were black like the car itself so Mr Small couldn't see if anyone was actually inside it. But as he passed through the gates of the park, a smart chauffeur in a purple uniform stepped out of the car and quickly opened one of the back doors. Immediately a small bald man in a brightly-coloured check suit bounced out and ran over.

"If you're from the newspapers or the telly, it's too early for an interview," said Mr Small, walking into the tent. The other man scampered after him and, in an accent that Mr Small recognised as American, he endeavoured to explain himself:

"No no no. You don't understand," he began. "My name is Darius Finkle."

It was dark inside the tent. The man called Finkle screwed up his eyes and peered into the gloom. He looked across and saw Kim's mountainous frame lying peacefully sleeping.

"Wow!" he exclaimed. "That your daughter? Gee! What a gal!"

Hearing voices, Kim rolled over and opened her eyes.

"Morning, Dad," she smiled sleepily.

"Good morning, Kim," said Mr Small. "I've brought you a cuppa."

He handed her the bucket and she began to drink.

"Fantastic! Fan-tastic!" continued Mr Finkle.

Mr Small was getting a bit irritated by the stranger.

"Look, what exactly can I do for you, Mr

Winkle or whatever your name is?"

"Finkle! Finkle!" laughed the man. "And it's not what *you* can do for *me*, it's what *I* can do for *you*!"

Mr Small frowned. "What exactly can you do for me, then?" he asked warily.

"My dear man," beamed Mr Finkle. "I am the managing director of ACE."

"ACE?" said Mr Small. "What's ACE when it's at home?"

"You mean you've never heard of the **A**cme **C**lothes **E**mporium?" gasped Mr Finkle. "Why, we make more T-shirts and trainers than any other company in the world. From Boston to Bangkok, from Mile End to Mandalay, kids everywhere are getting kitted out in ACE gear."

"Very interesting, I'm sure," said Mr Small, "but what's that got to do with me?"

Mr Finkle went on. "Why, when I saw your little gal on the six o'clock news, I said to my wife Mildred, 'Mildred,' I said, 'I bet that kid's gonna need a darned big outfit tomorrow.' And she turned to me and said, 'Well, Darius honey, you're the biggest guy in kids' clothes, so why don't you darn well do something about it.'"

Kim sat up and began to take notice as Mr Finkle continued his story.

"So I drove down to my factory and I got the folks down there working away all night to make me up the biggest set of ACE clothes in the world and I've got 'em right outside in the trunk of my car if you'll allow me to present 'em to you all."

Kim's face lit up with excitement.

"Brilliant!" she beamed.

"Well, I'm not sure," said Mr Small. "I don't think we can afford anything fancy like that."

"My dear man, I don't want any money!" laughed Mr Finkle. "The publicity I'll get from

Kim wearing my label will be ample reward, I assure you. Hey, you all wait here while I go and get my man Bernie to bring 'em in."

And with that, Darius Finkle scampered out of the tent.

"Well, what a piece of luck," said Mr Small. "Now at least you'll have something big enough to wear."

"I can't wait to see what Mr Finkle's brought me," said Kim.

Wrapping herself in sheets and blankets, she stood up. As she did, Mr Small's smile evaporated immediately. He could see at once that his daughter had grown even bigger during the night. She was now approximately twenty feet high.

"Well, let's just hope that this new outfit is really going to be big enough," he sighed.

Mr Finkle reappeared, followed by Bernie, who struggled to carry in the new set of clothes. Mr Finkle had indeed thought of everything. There was a huge pair of pants and socks, a large T-shirt, a vast track suit top and trousers, an enormous pair of trainers and to top off the bright yellow outfit, a massive baseball cap.

"Cor! Look at that!" exclaimed Mr Small.

"Each of those trainers is the size of a small canoe and that cap's as big as a boy scouts' tent. Let's just hope they fit."

But Mr Finkle was quite confident. He explained that he'd fed all the information about Kim's growth rate into his personal computer which had calculated quite correctly that Kim would reach twenty feet tall by the following morning and he'd had the clothes made up to that specification. He was right. They fitted Kim to perfection.

"Oh they're great!" she beamed. "Thank you, Mr Finkle. Thank you."

"Well, thank you, little lady, for wearing them," he grinned. "When the kids round the world see you looking pretty as a picture they're gonna want their moms and dads to buy them a set of ACE clothes too. Ooo-ee!"

Mr Finkle, Mr Small and Kim stepped out of the Big Top into the bright sunshine.

"Gee, what a swell day," smiled Mr Finkle walking towards his car. "What are you folks doing with yourselves?"

"Well," began Kim, "Mr Pottle, the man who lent us the tent, is having a funfair on the common and Dad's taking me and Kevin along."

"Well, you guys have a good day, and if there's anything else I can do, just get on the phone and give a quick tinkle to Darius Finkle. 'Bye now."

Mr Finkle climbed back into his car, and like a long black shark the limousine glided off down the street.

8

All the Fun of the Fair

After breakfast (which for Kim consisted of a washing-up bowl full of cornflakes and twenty pieces of toast), the Smalls set off for the fair. They went in Mr Small's lorry, Kevin sitting in the cab next to his dad and Kim stretched out in the back. As they drove through the South London streets, people everywhere pointed and

waved. Kim had become a celebrity. She'd been on television, she'd been in the newspapers, there was no doubt about it... she was famous. As shoppers shrieked and children cheered, Kim waved back happily but Kevin slumped down gloomily into his seat hating Kim getting all the fuss and wishing all this rotten business had never happened.

When they eventually arrived, the common was a kaleidoscope of colour. There were bundles of balloons, furiously flashing lights and gaudily painted stalls stuffed with soft toys of every description. The air was thick with the smell of onions and the ground vibrated to the throbbing bass of the disco beat. Mr Small parked his lorry on the grass and they climbed out.

"I want an ice cream," said Kevin, "and a balloon and a go on the bumper cars and the helter skelter and..."

"Slow down! Slow down!" said Mr Small. "There's plenty of time for everything."

Kevin had a great time at the fair. He went on every ride – the ghost train, the roundabouts, the big dipper. He tried his luck at the darts, the hoopla and the rifle range. He consumed a toffee apple, a hamburger and a candy floss and it was the first time for days that anyone had seen him smile.

Kim, because of her enormous size, couldn't really go on any of the rides. She did win a coconut on the test your strength game, although she banged the hammer down so hard that the lead weight shot up and seriously dented the bell.

The Smalls met lots of people they knew at the fair like Stacey and Tracey (Kim's best friends from school), Billy Wilkinson (who kept right out

of their way) and Dr Patel from the hospital.

"I'm still working on the antidote to make your daughter shrink," she explained to Mr Small. "I'm almost there but I'm missing one vital ingredient."

"Well, keep trying, Doc," said Mr Small. "I'm sure you'll crack it eventually."

It wasn't long before Kevin ran out of rides to go on. The only thing he hadn't tried was the inflatable.

For some reason the huge yellow and red castle lay spread out flat on the grass and a very anxious-looking Perry Pottle stood staring down at it, a look of despair on his usually cheery face. Nearby, three of his workers tried in vain to get the electric air pump working.

"Cheer up," said Mr Small, "can't be that bad."

"It is that bad, Ken," sighed Perry Pottle. "Flippin' pump's packed up. No one can get the bloomin' thing working. No pump... no inflatable!"

"Oh, what a swizz!" moaned Kevin. "I was looking forward to that most of all."

"So were a lot of other kids," sighed Perry

Pottle sadly. "If only there was some other way of blowing it up."

Everybody stood about looking gloomy and feeling as flat as the deflated cushion of air. Suddenly Kim's face lit up.

"Er... Mr Pottle," she began. "I've got an idea."

"What's that, love?" asked the circus man.

"Well, I was just wondering... I know it sounds silly but... could I have a go at blowing up the inflatable for you?"

There was a stunned silence from all around. Suddenly Perry Pottle leaped in the air, his eyes twinkling wildly.

"Wonderful, my dear! Wonderful! What a wonderful wonderful idea!"

He led Kim over and showed her the tube where the air went in. Kim lifted the tube to her mouth, puffed out her cheeks and began to blow. She blew and blew and blew and blew. The crowd gasped. The inflatable began to grow and grow and grow and grow. The towers of the huge castle filled with air and the castle popped upright and within minutes the big bouncy cushion of air was ready to use. The people went

berserk, clapping, cheering and throwing their hats in the air.

"She's done it!" cried Perry Pottle. "What a girl!"

"Well done, Kim," called Mr Small. "Go on, Kevin lad. Say thanks to your sister. You can go on the inflatable now."

For once, Kevin had to admit that having a giant in the family did have its advantages. "Thanks," he mumbled reluctantly. Then he climbed up for a bounce followed by Stacey and Tracey and a dozen other happy children.

"Well, you've saved the day, Kim," smiled Perry Pottle. "Are you sure you wouldn't like to come and join my circus?"

9

Theo Thugg

The next day was Sunday. All the excitement and drama of the last forty-eight hours had quite exhausted Mr Small and he had decided to have a nice long lie-in.

Unfortunately, at 8.30 a.m. the phone began to ring. Mr Small tried to ignore it. He put his head under the pillow and pretended not to hear. The phone rang on. Mr Small curled up under the duvet willing the nasty noise to stop but the phone rang and rang and rang until he could stand it no longer. Grumpily he hauled himself out of bed and crossly thumped downstairs. He snatched the receiver and held it to his ear. An unfamiliar voice began to speak.

"Ah, you're up. Good. The name's Thugg. Theo Thugg. You've probably heard of me..."

"I've never heard of you," yawned Mr Small. "Who are you?"

After a stunned silence, the voice on the phone

continued. "You must have heard of me! I'm Theo Thugg! The producer of *Splodge*. You must have heard of *Splodge*?"

"Oh yeah, *Splodge*," answered Mr Small taking an interest. "The kids' TV programme. My boy Kevin never misses your show. He'd do anything to win a *Splodge* badge. He was just saying..."

Cutting Mr Small off in mid-sentence, Mr Thugg continued.

"It's about that extraordinary daughter of yours, Kim. We'd like her to be on the show tomorrow. If you could bring her along to the studios at say three o'clock...?"

Mr Small was glowing with excitement. "Oh thank you, Mr Thugg. Kim will be delighted. She's always wanted to..."

There was a click on the end of the phone. Theo Thugg was a busy busy man and had no time to chat with the likes of Ken Small.

Kevin came downstairs rubbing his eyes. "Who was that?" he yawned.

"That," announced Mr Small grandly, "was none other than Theo Thugg!"

Kevin looked quite blank.

"Who the heck's Theo Thugg?"

"You don't know Theo Thugg?" gasped Mr Small in mock amazement. "He's the producer of your favourite television show – *Splodge*!"

"*Splodge*?" spluttered Kevin. "The producer of *Splodge* phoning *here*! I knew it! They got my letter. At last! They want *me* on the show. They want to see my model of Tower Bridge made entirely out of dry spaghetti. Yippee! I'm going to be on the telly. I'm going to be a star!"

Kevin began jumping up and down for joy. He was so excited he jumped over the banisters and gave the cat a big kiss on the head.

"Hang on, son, take it easy," interrupted Mr Small. "I don't know quite how to tell you this. You see... er... well it's not *you* that they want on the programme. It's... uh... Kim."

The colour seemed to drain from Kevin's face. His whole body went limp as he flopped down on to the stairs. He appeared to be suffering from severe shock.

"They don't want *me*?" he mumbled. "They don't want to see my spaghetti model? They want to see Kim???"

Before Mr Small could comfort him, Kevin leapt to his feet and began to bawl his eyes out, huge tears plopping down on to his pyjama sleeve as he tried to hide his face.

"It's not fair!" he sobbed. "It's just not fair! It's never me! Always her! Ever since she became big, people are always fussing over her! Kim this! Kim that! Kim the other! Nobody cares about me! Nobody takes any notice of me! I might as well not be here! It's just Kim flippin' Kong all day long!" And with that outburst Kevin rushed upstairs, slamming the bedroom door behind him.

10

Splodge!

On Monday, Mr Small collected Kim from school after lunch so that they would have plenty of time to get to the *Splodge* studios for the show. An hour later they arrived at the NIT Centre or **N**etwork **I**nternational **T**elevision as the sign said over the gate.

Mr Small parked his lorry in the car park and he and Kim headed across to the main building. Waiting in the reception area was a tense-looking man with a twitchy moustache.

"Theo Thugg," he announced. "You must be the Smalls. Right, follow me. Come along, come along. Have to get straight back to the studio. They can't cope without me. Hurry, hurry!"

The celebrated producer scuttled off round the back of the building and led them through enormous studio doors on to the set of *Splodge*. Kim blinked when she saw the hundreds of coloured spotlights illuminating the familiar

Splodge sofa. She immediately recognised the three smiley faces of the *Splodge* presenters, Ziggy (with the pink glasses), Wiggy (with the pink hair) and Arthur wearing a pink boiler suit.

"Fab to have you here," chuckled Ziggy.

"Brill," giggled Wiggy.

"Fantasticola!" laughed Arthur.

"That's enough chit chat," snapped Theo Thugg. "We've got a show to do here."

He started to flick through his script and bark out orders as he explained what was happening in the programme.

"Now, first off Ziggy's going to bake an upside-down banana cake. Then we've got an update on the old sock appeal. Next Wiggy's going to interview Kim Small. Then Arthur's going to demonstrate how to manicure an elephant's toenail and the bagpipe band will play us out. Got that everyone?"

The assorted camera operators, sound engineers and lighting crew scratched their heads, grunted and went off to get ready. Mr Small and Kim went to sit in the corner of the studio and waited for the show to begin.

"Cor, this is exciting, isn't it?" said Mr Small. "I've never been in a TV studio before."

"I can't believe I'm going to be on telly," said Kim. "But I do feel sorry for Kevin. I wish he'd have come with us. He'd have loved seeing all this."

"I asked him to come," said Mr Small. "But he said if he couldn't actually be on the programme with his spaghetti model then he didn't want to know about it."

At that moment the studio door opened and an enormous wooden crate was wheeled in. On the side of the crate were stencilled the words LONDON ZOO.

"That must be the elephant," said Mr Small.

A keeper in a green uniform unfastened the

padlock and let down the side of the crate. He went inside and returned a second later leading out an extremely nervous-looking elephant. The poor creature took one look at the lights and the cameras and all the people, gave a loud bellowing trumpet and rushed back into the crate to hide.

"Get that animal back out immediately!" screamed Theo Thugg. "The show starts in two minutes."

Several of the bagpipe band who had just arrived, wearing their kilts and sporrans, rushed over to help the zoo keeper push the elephant out of the crate. The terrified beast stood trembling at the side of the set.

The studio doors slammed shut. The red ON THE AIR lights began to flash.

"We'll be on in thirty seconds," called the floor manager. "Twenty... Fifteen... Ten... Five... Four... Three... Two... One... Action!"

Suddenly the jolly *Splodge* theme came blaring out of the speakers. They were on the air.

"Hi!" beamed Ziggy into camera one, "and welcome to another fun-packed programme. Later on, we'll be meeting our celebrity guest Kim Small but first, have you ever fancied baking an upside-down banana cake for your granny?"

Kim sat in the corner fascinated as she watched Ziggy beating the batter and bashing the bananas as he threw everything into his culinary creation. It really looked rather tasty and it made Kim feel quite hungry. She licked her lips then suddenly winced. It was that loose tooth of hers again. It had been wobbling away for several days and as it swung from side to side, it really felt ready to drop out. But there wasn't time to worry about that now, there was too much going on. Arthur was standing in front of an enormous mountain of old socks, thanking the viewers for having sent in over two million items of discarded footwear. He explained that every little sock counted and they would all go to support the *Splodge* Save a Slug Appeal.

Before Kim realised what was happening, she heard Wiggy making an announcement to Camera 3.

"And now... we're delighted to have on the show... you've all seen her on the news and in the papers... she's the biggest little girl in the world – Kim Small!"

"Go on, love..." whispered Mr Small. "Good

luck." Kim strode forward, ducking under the boom mike as she stepped from the shadows into the bright lights.

"Welcome to *Splodge*," smiled Wiggy. "I won't ask you to sit down 'cos you might break the sofa. Ha ha ha ha ha! No, but seriously, Kim, tell us what it's like to be twenty feet tall."

Kim was suddenly feeling terrified about being on the television. Her hands felt wet and clammy. Her tongue felt dry and dusty. She nervously started to lick her lips. She opened her mouth to answer Wiggy's question but before she could utter a word something terrible happened. Her loose tooth that had been hanging around, waiting to drop out for days, suddenly chose that precise moment to work itself free and fall out.

Now remember that Kim being as big as she was, meant that her tooth was the size and weight of a small paving stone. It came crashing down on to the table where Ziggy had been doing his cooking. It hit the end of the table with such force that the whole thing tipped up like a seesaw and Ziggy's upside-down banana cake was sent hurtling across the studio like a bullet from a gun. With a great SPLAATTT! the cake hit the elephant straight in the face. The startled creature let out a terrified roar, and breaking free from its keeper, thundered on to the set sending the bagpipe band scattering in every direction. The animal made straight towards the mountain of socks...

THUD!

The elephant crashed right through the middle, sending socks flying in every direction – red socks, bedsocks, short socks, sport socks, spotty socks, grotty socks – like a great multicoloured sock storm. People were screaming and running to take cover. Ziggy was hiding behind the sofa. Wiggy had climbed on top of a camera. Arthur had been buried by an avalanche of smelly socks. In the control room, Theo Thugg was banging his head against the desk.

"This is a nightmare!" he sobbed. "I'm ruined! Ruined!"

The situation in the studio was looking dangerous. The elephant was running amok, knocking over spotlights and trampling down the scenery. Nobody could do anything about it. If it went on much longer there would surely be a terrible accident. There was only one person

strong enough to stop a rampaging elephant and that person was Kim Small. By now the elephant had completely demolished the set. In a mad frenzy the terrified beast had squashed the sofa, crushed the cameras and mangled the microphones.

Kim sprang into action. She'd never had any dealings with elephants before but she did have a way with cats. When she wanted to comfort her pet cat Sam, she would hold him in her arms, give him a cuddle and tickle him under the neck. And that's exactly what she did to the startled elephant.

The elephant had never been picked up before and no one had ever tried to tickle him under the tusks. At first he struggled and strained, wriggled and roared and wrapped his trunk firmly around Kim's neck. But after a minute he found that he quite liked being tickled and he began to relax, lying back in Kim's arms and enjoying the sensation.

"There, there," cooed Kim comfortingly. "Who's a happy little elephant then? Who's a jolly little jumbo? Oochy coochy coochy coo..."

Gently rocking the pacified pachyderm in her

arms and softly stroking his ears, Kim carried the elephant across the studio floor and popped him carefully back into his crate, where he stood and gazed up at her lovingly.

The keeper rushed over and snapped on the padlock. "I never seen nothing like that before!" he chuckled. "That was bloomin' marvellous. Any time you want to come and work at the zoo, my girl, the job's yours."

Now that the danger was over, people began to emerge from their hiding places and congratulate Kim. Arthur crawled out from under a huge pile of socks and looked into Camera 3 (the only one still working) to make the final announcement:

"Well, that's all from *Splodge* for today," he panted. "But don't forget we'll be back tomorrow for a *Splodge* special when we'll be doing a live broadcast from Big Ben in London. So until then, byyyye!"

The dishevelled and depleted bagpipe band burst into a spirited but shaky rendition of *Nelly the Elephant* and the credits began to roll. The show was over.

In the sitting room of 37 Park Road, Kevin Small stabbed at the remote control and the TV screen went dead.

"I'll show them," he muttered defiantly. "I'll just show them! Kim's not the only one who can be on the telly. She's not the only one who can do brave stunts. Oh no. Oh no."

Kevin stood up, kicked the sofa and stomped out of the sitting room, slamming the door shut behind him.

11

Big Ben

Kevin Small had a big plan. He was going to be on television one way or another. He was going to be a celebrity, a famous face, a star! His idea was simple but bold. He knew that the *Splodge* Team was going to do a live broadcast from Big Ben, so he decided that he would travel to Westminster and as soon as the TV cameras began filming the enormous clock, he would leap over the wall and climb up the side of the building. It would be stunning, a smash, a sensation! Everybody would be watching. All the cameras would be on *him*. People would stop and ask, "Who is that brave boy climbing up the side of Big Ben?" And other people would answer, "Why that's none other than Kevin Small." Everyone would marvel at how breathtakingly daring he was. At last people would take notice of him and not witter on about how marvellous Kim was.

So on Tuesday afternoon, as soon as the school bell went for home time, Kevin walked calmly out of the playground, got on a bus and travelled to Parliament Square. When he got off the bus, there was Big Ben towering above him. Kevin crossed the road and saw four big blue vans parked at the foot of the building. Each van had NIT in bold white letters painted on the side. The television crew were rushing about with cables and microphones, spotlights and cameras.

In the middle of all this activity, Theo Thugg, with a plaster on his forehead, was barking at everyone to hurry up. In the back of one of the vans, Ziggy, Wiggy and Arthur were having their make-up applied. In one hour the live broadcast

would begin. When it did, Kevin would start his climb.

A few miles away, Kim stood waiting by the school gates. By now everyone had gone and the school keeper was already locking up. Kim walked home on her own and found her dad waiting anxiously outside the house.

"Where have you been?" he asked. "And where's Kevin?"

"I don't know," said Kim. "I waited for ages but he didn't show up."

"Hmpf!" snorted Mr Small. "He's been acting very strangely since we got back from the studios yesterday, all sulky and secretive. I just hope he's not going to be awkward. I'll phone up a few of his pals and see if he's gone round to play at someone's house."

Mr Small went into the house and switched on the television for Kim who crouched in the front garden, peering through the sitting room window at the screen. Mr Small phoned four of Kevin's friends without any luck. He was just about to call a fifth when a screech from Kim made him drop the phone and come running to see what was wrong.

"Look, Dad! Look!" cried Kim jabbing a huge finger towards the TV set. Mr Small stared, puzzled at the picture.

The *Splodge Special* had just begun, but the show was obviously not going to plan. Ziggy, Wiggy and Arthur were in a particularly excitable state as they gabbled incoherently and pointed upwards to what appeared to be a tiny speck on the side of Big Ben. In the background the wailing sirens of fire engines and police cars could be heard.

As the camera zoomed in closer, Mr Small and Kim could make out a small figure climbing up the side of the building.

"What a crazy stunt!" muttered Mr Small shaking his head. "Some people! Huh!"

With a shake, the camera went in even closer. They could now see that the adventurous climber was a boy. On the ground, Ziggy was blowing a gasket.

"Yes, yes, it's a boy! A young boy! He appears to be climbing the side of the great clock! We have no idea why! It's amazing! Incredible! Fantasticola!"

At that moment, the penny dropped.

"Strewth!" cried Mr Small. "That's our Kevin!"

"Kevin?" gasped Kim. "What's he doing up Big Ben?"

"I don't know," cried Mr Small, "but we'd better get along there double quick. Come on!"

Mr Small sprinted up the garden path, leapt into the cab of his lorry and turned the key. Kim jumped up on the back and held tight.

"Ready," she called. "Let's go!"

But nothing happened. Mr Small turned the key again. The engine gave a cough and a splutter then nothing. He tried once more. The lorry shuddered and shook, lurched forward then stopped dead in the middle of the road.

"It's packed up!" cried Mr Small in despair. "What a time to choose!"

He jumped down from the cab, stuck his head under the bonnet and began to fiddle around with the engine. Kim climbed down from the back.

"There's no time for that, Dad," she called. "Come on, I'll give you a lift."

Before Mr Small could answer, Kim reached down, scooped him up in the palm of her hand and hoisted him up on to her shoulder.

"Hold tight," she said. "Big Ben here we come!"

12

Hooray for the Hero!

The higher Kevin climbed, the more people gathered at the foot of Big Ben to watch him. There were clicks and snaps and flashes as visitors from every part of the world pointed their cameras up at the daring young climber.

A police officer with a megaphone was leaning out of a helicopter begging the foolhardy boy to come down. Fire engines extended their longest ladders but Kevin had now climbed so high that none of them reached anywhere near him. The TV cameras went on filming. The crowd went on cheering. Theo Thugg was being carried on a stretcher into the back of an ambulance.

Kevin was happy. He adored all the attention. He loved everyone looking at him. He had reached the huge white clock face and he stopped to rest. He turned to admire the view. The River Thames lay stretched out like a sparkling ribbon

before him. There were the historic Houses of Parliament, Westminster Abbey, and tiny toy cars and people scuttling about like ants. He felt on top of the world. He was above it all like some sort of king... King Kevin. He liked the sound of it.

But suddenly he saw something that jolted him back to reality. On legs the size of telegraph poles, his sister Kim was sprinting across Westminster Bridge towards him. Leaping over cars, brushing past treetops and hurdling police barriers, she was advancing ever nearer.

Kevin's heart sank. He felt his moment of glory was coming to an end. At that moment he suddenly lost his concentration and slipped. The crowd let out a terrified gasp. As Kevin began to topple from his perch his hands scrambled to grab on to something. As he started to fall his fingers made a frantic grab for the massive minute hand of the clock. He caught hold of it just in time and hung there dangling dangerously in space. This wasn't fun any more.

"HELP!" he screamed. "GET ME DOWN! I WANNA COME DOWN! HELP!"

By now Kim had reached the foot of Big Ben.

Mr Small clung on to her shoulder shouting instructions into her ear.

At her spectacular arrival, all the cameras suddenly turned from Kevin on to Kim and a thousand flashes were aimed in her direction.

"What's going on here, then?" asked the Chief of Police. "I've got enough on my plate as it is!"

"That's my brother up there," panted Kim, "and I'm going up to get him down!"

"Kim! You can't!" cried Mr Small. "It's too dangerous!"

Kim lifted her dad from her shoulder and placed him gently on the ground beside Ziggy, Wiggy and Arthur.

"I've got to save him, Dad," she said. "It's the only way."

Before anyone could stop her (and who could have stopped her anyway?) Kim bounded forward and began to climb up the side of Big Ben.

Far above her Kevin was all in. His arms felt like lumps of lead. His fingers ached. His stomach was churning. Tears were streaming down his face.

"I can't hang on much longer," he sobbed.

Slowly, oh so slowly he began to feel himself

slipping. Kim was halfway up the side of the building and climbing at a most fantastic pace. If Kevin could hold on for a few seconds more...

At that moment there was a loud CLUNK as the clock hand Kevin was clinging on to shunted on another minute. It was a quarter past five and as always on the quarter hour, the chimes of Big Ben began to ring out. BOING BOING BOING BOING – BOING BOING BOING BOING. The bells were deafening to Kevin. They hurt his ears. He couldn't bear it any longer. Suddenly his fingers slipped. He struggled to regain his hold but it was no good. He let out a terrifying scream as he plummetted downwards.

"AAAAARGHHHHHH!"

Kim looked up and saw her brother hurtling towards her. It looked as if she was too late. But no! In a split second she snatched the cap from her head and held it outstretched in front of her. With a WHOOOSH and a BOINNNGGG Kevin bounced into the huge hat and was saved.

The crowd went bananas. They shouted and whistled and cheered.

"Well done, Kim!"

"What a girl!"

"She's a hero!"

Kevin lay stretched out on his back inside Kim's enormous cap. He couldn't believe he was still alive. He looked up and saw his sister beaming down at him, a huge gap-toothed smile on her face.

"Oh Kim," he cried. "You saved me! You saved me!"

"It's all right, Kevin," she said. "It's all over now. We'll be down soon."

Clutching the cap and Kevin carefully in one

hand, Kim climbed down the side of Big Ben and back to safety. Everybody was ecstatic. Mr Small hugged Kevin. Ziggy hugged Wiggy. Arthur hugged the Chief of Police.

"Oh, I've been such a twit," sobbed Kevin. "I've caused so much trouble. And all because I was jealous of Kim and all the attention and fuss she's been getting." He looked up at his huge sister and hugged her knee.

"I'm sorry, Kim," he said solemnly. "I've been so horrible to you. You're the best sister in the world. Can you ever forgive me?"

"'Course I can," smiled Kim, and she bent down and gave her brother a big sloppy kiss on the head.

Dr Patel suddenly emerged from the back of an ambulance where she'd been attending to Theo Thugg. "Hello, Mr Small," she smiled.

"Is he all right?" asked Mr Small peering in at the distraught producer.

"It's just not his week," replied the doctor. "He worries too much and works too hard. And talking of work, I need to talk to you about the antidote I've been working on."

Mr Small looked around at the chaotic scene –

the television cameras, the crowds and the noise.

"We can't talk here," he said. "Why don't you come back home for a cup of tea and we'll have a nice cosy chat about it there?"

13

Tea and Sympathy

Back at Park Road Mr Small and Dr Patel sat in the back garden sipping their tea.

"Another biscuit, Dr Patel?" asked Mr Small.

"Call me Poppy," said the doctor.

"Then you must call me Ken," smiled Mr Small.

"You have some beautiful flowers, Ken," remarked the doctor. "So colourful."

"Yes, it's my hobby, gardening," said Mr

Small. Then his face dropped as he remembered something.

"Of course it's because of gardening and that awful *Gro-Kwik* mixture that poor old Kim's in the state she is."

"Well," said Dr Patel, "as you know I've been working for days trying to come up with a solution that will bring Kim back to her normal size."

"Any luck yet?" asked Mr Small hopefully.

Dr Patel sighed and shook her head.

"I'm afraid not. I'm almost there, I know I am. I need one more ingredient but I just can't work out what that ingredient is."

Mr Small offered her another biscuit. "Don't feel bad about it," he said. "You're trying the best you can. You'll get there in the end. I know you will."

"I hope so," replied the doctor. "Look, I'd better go now. I'm going to do a bit more work in the lab tonight. Who knows, I might just strike lucky."

Dr Patel stood up.

"Hang on, Poppy," said Mr Small rushing across the garden. He began to pick some beautiful purple flowers. When he had a fine bunch he came back over and presented them to Dr Patel.

"Oh they're lovely, Ken," she said. "Thank you so much."

"Just a little something to say thanks for what you're trying to do for Kim. We do appreciate it you know."

That night Mr Small came over to the Big Top to say goodnight to Kim. He was shocked to find her curled up on the big bed crying her eyes out.

"What's the matter, love?" asked Mr Small. "Kevin hasn't been annoying you, has he?"

"No, it's not that," sniffed Kim. "Kevin's being really nice to me now."

"What is it then? What's upsetting you?"

He took out his pocket handkerchief to dry Kim's face but realised immediately that he could have really done with something the size of a tablecloth.

"I don't think I'll ever be ordinary again," sobbed Kim. "I'll probably be a huge great monster for the rest of my life."

"Don't say that," said Mr Small reassuringly. "Now what's brought all this on?"

"I heard Dr Patel say she hadn't found a cure for me yet," sobbed Kim and great bucket-sized tears plopped down on to the ground, soaking her dad's shoes.

"Steady on, love," said Mr Small. "It's just a matter of time. We just have to be patient, that's all."

Kim remained unconvinced.

"But what if we wait and wait and Dr Patel never manages to find an antidote? What then?"

Mr Small tenderly stroked his daughter's hair.

"Even if you never get small again I'll still love you just as much. Whatever size you are, you're still my little girl. Now, stop fretting, and get some sleep. You've got school in the morning."

He leant over and gave Kim a kiss.

"Goodnight, love," he said. "By the way, I put your tooth under the pillow. You could always ask the tooth fairy to make you small again."

"Goodnight, Dad," smiled Kim, shutting her eyes. "I think I might just try that."

14

The Shrinking Solution

In the middle of the night Mr Small was woken by the phone ringing. Bleary-eyed, he staggered out of bed and down the stairs.

"If that's Theo Thugg again I'll... I'll..."

He lifted the receiver and put it to his ear.

"Hello!" he snapped gruffly.

Much to his surprise it was Dr Patel's excited voice that he heard.

"Ken!" she shrieked. "Eureka! I've done it!"

"W...w... what are you on about?" he gasped.

"I've done it!" she repeated. "The shrinking solution! I've got it! I'm coming right over!"

With a click Dr Patel hung up, leaving Mr Small standing there in his pyjamas, quite flummoxed. He rushed upstairs and got dressed.

Kevin had woken up and was anxious to know what was going on.

"Dr Patel's made some sort of medicine stuff that she reckons will make Kim small again," explained Mr Small.

"Great!" said Kevin. He too got dressed and they hurried out to the Big Top to tell Kim the good news.

Ten minutes later Dr Patel arrived in her car. From out of the boot she brought a large bell jar full of some mysterious purple liquid.

"Is that it?" asked Mr Small curiously.

"That's it!" beamed Dr Patel. "The shrink drink. And it's all thanks to you, Ken, that I found my final ingredient."

"Me?" exclaimed Mr Small. "What did I do?"

The doctor flashed him a broad smile.

"When I was here this afternoon you gave me

some beautiful flowers from your garden."

"Yes..."

"Well, I took them back with me and I was curious to find out exactly what type of flowers they were."

"Oh, I could have told you that," said Mr Small. "They're violets."

Dr Patel smiled knowingly.

"Yes, they're violets, but not ordinary violets. I looked them up in a botanical book. The Latin name for that particular strain is Violetta Shrinkanis."

"I don't know anything about Latin names," said Mr Small.

The doctor continued. "Roughly translated Violetta Shrinkanis means shrinking violet."

"Shrinking violet!" gasped Kevin. "You don't mean...?"

"Yes, I *do* mean," said Dr Patel. "Those flowers contain a chemical that has shrinking properties."

Mr Small was stunned into silence as he struggled to understand.

"So you mean my violets are all mixed up in this jar then?"

"Exactly," said the doctor. "When I discovered the flowers were shrinking violets I diluted them into the solution I'd made and they turned out to be the very missing ingredient I'd been searching for."

Kim could only utter one word. "Wow!"

"Well, what are we waiting for?" laughed Mr Small, pouring the big bottle of liquid into the plastic bucket that Kim used for a cup. He handed the bucket up to her.

"Go on, love," he said. "Down the hatch."

"Drink it up," cried Kevin.

"Good luck," called Dr Patel.

Kim lifted the bucket to her lips and began to drink.

"Glub!... glub!... glub!"

She drained the bucket with one mighty swig then licked her lips.

"Quite nice," she smiled. "A bit fizzy... and fruity."

"Anything happening yet?" asked Dr Patel anxiously.

Kim shook her head. The drink didn't seem to be having any effect at all.

"Oh, it's not working!" sighed Mr Small.

"Give it a chance, Dad," said Kevin.

Suddenly Kim's eyes opened as wide as dinner plates and she began to make a strange moaning sound.

"Oooooooooh!"

Something was starting to happen. Something strange was taking place inside Kim's twenty-foot frame. It was similar to when Kim had drunk the *Gro-Kwik* mixture, but this time in reverse. At first she felt freezing cold then burning hot then cold then hot then cold again. This was followed by a gushing, rushing, fuzzy, muzzy, belchy, squelchy, slurpy, burby sensation then a terrible scratching and itching all over the inside of her body ending up with a curious prickly tickly tingly pins and needley feeling all down her spine.

"What's going on?" asked Kevin.

"She's still the same size!" said Mr Small gloomily.

"Give it a chance!" cried Dr Patel.

Suddenly Kim let out a huge "HIC!" It was so fierce that the whole of the Big Top shuddered and shook. The antidote had begun to work.

"Look!" cried Kevin. "She's getting smaller!"

"It worked! It worked!" shouted Dr Patel.

"Hooray!" shrieked Mr Small.

It was the most peculiar sensation Kim had ever experienced. Second by second she was shrinking in size. Her head no longer brushed the top of the tent. When she looked down, the ground seemed to be getting closer and closer. Her enormous clothes were becoming much too big and were starting to hang off her.

"Well done, Poppy!" laughed Mr Small shaking the doctor's hand. "I knew you'd do it."

Kim was down to fifteen feet and shrinking rapidly.

"That's the way, Kim!" called Kevin encouragingly.

Kim was down to ten feet tall and still going strong. In less than a minute she was back to her proper normal size again. Mr Small rushed forward to hug her.

"How do you feel, love?" he asked.

"I still feel a bit tingly," answered Kim.

"Oh, I'm so happy to have you back like this," cried Mr Small and he gave her another big hug.

But then a look of horror spread across Mr Small's face.

"Hang on!" he shrieked. "You're getting smaller!"

Dr Patel gasped. Kevin's mouth dropped open.

It was true. Before their very eyes Kim was getting smaller and smaller and smaller. By now she was the size of a Sindy doll and still shrinking. Mr Small got down on his knees to talk to his tiny daughter.

"Kim!" he cried. "Are you all right? For heaven's sake, say something!"

Kim looked up at her dad. Slowly a smile spread across her miniature face and her tiny eyes twinkled. "Oh, Dad," she piped softly, "here we go again!"